SOPHIE the CHATTERBOX

Finding the right name isn't easy!
See what else Sophie tries out. . . .

SOPHIE the CHATTERBOX

by Lara Bergen

illustrated by Laura Tallardy

SCHOLASTIC INC.

New York Toronto London Auckland
Sydney Mexico City New Delhi Hong Kong

To Stu, for keeping me honest

ISBN 978-0-545-14606-7

12 11 10 9 8 7 6 5 4 3 2 1   10 11 12 13 14 15/0

Printed in the U.S.A.   40
First printing, October 2010
Designed by Tim Hall

CHAPTER 1

Sophie was so happy! And not just because she was going on a field trip. (She really, really, *really* loved those.) Sophie was also happy because she had a perfect new name. A name that made her special. A name that said it all!

"Don't call me Sophie M. anymore. Just call me Sophie the Honest!" she told her best friend, Kate Barry, as they climbed onto the field trip bus.

Ms. Moffly's third-grade class was going to see where George Washington was born! It was nice to know that something special had happened close to Ordinary, Virginia, where Sophie lived.

Sometimes Sophie thought it was the most boring place in the whole wide world.

Sophie used to also think she was the most boring girl in the whole world.

But not anymore!

Not since she told Ms. Moffly the truth about stealing the fifth graders' snake. Now she was sure that she was the most honest kid in her whole class. Maybe the whole school!

"By the way, Kate," Sophie went on. "Have I told you, *honestly*, that you're my very best friend ever?"

Kate grinned. "Right back at you!"

Sophie smiled and grabbed Kate's hand. Then she pulled her down the aisle to the last row of the bus. That was their favorite row to sit in, mostly because it bumped so much.

But there was a problem when they got there.

The very back seats were already full. And what they were full of was Toby and Archie.

Toby Myers and Archie Dolan were the worst boys in their class. Sophie knew that for a fact.

They were very loud and very Yucky (with a capital "Yuck"). And they were taking up both back seats, even though they knew that Sophie and Kate liked to sit there.

That made them even worse!

Sophie was used to this, of course. Toby was always bugging her somehow. Usually she acted like she did not care, but today she could not do that. She was Sophie the Honest, after all!

"I have to be honest," she said to Toby. "This disappoints me very much."

Toby smiled a big smile. "Good!" he said. Then he stuck out his tongue.

Archie laughed.

But Sophie was not done being honest yet.

"This also makes me want to pinch you," she said.

Toby frowned and crossed his arms.

"But I won't," Sophie went on. "Because I don't want to get in trouble like I did last time. So instead, I'm going to sit down next to you. And Kate is going to sit down next to Archie."

"I *am*?" Kate said.

"You *are*?" said Toby and Archie.

"Yes," Sophie said to Kate, ignoring the boys. "Even though we don't want to. Because there's room. And because I know that they will hate that. And because if they don't let us, I'll tell Ms. Moffly." Sophie smiled. "And she will make them."

With that, Sophie sat down next to Toby. And she stuck out *her* tongue.

"Ew, gross! Girl cooties!" Toby cried. He jumped up on the seat and looked at Archie. "Come on. Let's move!" he said. "As far away from *them* as possible!"

A minute later, Sophie and Kate had not just one very back seat, but two! Still, they sat together. They were best friends, after all.

"I like you being Sophie the Honest!" Kate said.

They shared a high five.

Then Kate twisted her mouth. "Can I be honest?" she asked.

"Of course!" That seemed like a funny question to Sophie.

Kate shrugged. "It's just that 'Sophie the Honest'... I don't know... It's kind of a dull name. Don't you think?"

"Well, no...," Sophie said. Then she sighed. "Okay. Yes. Maybe."

To be honest, Sophie thought Kate was right. This name was not as exciting as "Sophie the Awesome" or "Sophie the Hero." Those were the two names Sophie had tried before. (Too bad they had not worked out as well as she'd hoped.)

But "Sophie the Honest" was still a good name. It made her special. And that was the point!

Plus it meant she could still wear the shirt she had on. She had made it when she was Sophie the Hero. It had a big *H* on the front. But *H* could be for "Hero" *or* "Honest"! And that was good, since her mom said not to write on shirts anymore.

"Maybe it's not an exciting name. But it is

important," Sophie told Kate. "Just think about George Washington!"

"What do you mean?" Kate asked.

"I mean, why was he so great?" Sophie said.

"Because he was our first president?" Kate guessed.

"No." Sophie shook her head. "Because he was so honest!" she said. "Remember when he cut down his father's cherry tree? And his father asked what happened, and George Washington said, 'I cannot tell a lie. I did it'?"

"No," Kate said. "But hey! Is that where he got his wooden teeth from?"

Sophie shrugged. "I don't know. But that's not my point. My point is that the story shows how important it is to tell the truth. They'll talk all about it on our field trip today, I bet!"

"Okay...," Kate said. But her mouth was still twisted.

Sophie sighed. "What?" she asked.

"Well," Kate said, "you're right. Telling the truth is important. But is it really such a big deal?

I mean, I tell the truth, too. Like right now." She grinned. "Your epidermis is showing!"

Sophie rolled her eyes. She had heard that joke before. (From Kate.) It meant that her *skin* was showing. She made a face.

"But can you tell the truth *all* the time?" Sophie asked her friend. "No matter what the *consequence* is?"

Sophie knew that was a hard question. She and Kate didn't like *consequences* very much.

She stood up. Then she yelled across the bus: "I cannot tell a lie. I left a banana peel on the lunchroom floor. On purpose!"

She sat back down and winked at Kate.

Then she heard her teacher's voice. "Who said that?" Ms. Moffly asked.

Sophie stood up again. "I did!" She waved her hand.

"Sophie Miller," said Ms. Moffly. She was standing at the front of the bus. And she was not alone.

Oops.

She was with Grace's mom. And Sydney's dad. They were the field trip chaperones. They were looking like moms and dads, crossing their arms and shaking their heads.

The kids in her class were looking like kids. They were all turned around, staring at her.

"I have to say, I am surprised by you," Ms. Moffly told Sophie. "If that's true, I think a consequence is in order. Don't you?"

Sophie nodded. Bring on the consequence! "Yes, Ms. Moffly," she said.

"You will stay in for recess tomorrow," Ms. Moffly told her. "Now turn around, everyone. Take a seat. It's time to go."

Sophie sighed and sat down. No recess? That was too bad. Sophie hadn't planned on *that* consequence.

She looked at Kate. "See? It's not so easy being honest," she said.

Kate patted her on the arm. "You are definitely Sophie the Honest!"

They felt the bus lurch forward. A round of

"On Top of Spaghetti" started up, but Sophie and Kate did not sing. Sophie was tired of that song, for one thing. Plus the "no recess" consequence was still sinking in.

And she had some more Sophie the Honest stuff to tell Kate.

"So, guess what? I am so honest, I even told my mom and dad about taking the fifth graders' snake. And that was before my big sister, Hayley, could say anything," Sophie said.

Kate looked a little surprised. And a lot impressed.

"Did you get in big trouble?" she asked Sophie.

Sophie grinned and shook her head.

"No! That's the best part," she said. "My mom and dad were so proud of me for being honest they didn't punish me or anything—just like George Washington's father!"

And that was not all Sophie had told her parents. She also told them about the squash stuck to the bottom of the dinner table (by her—every time they had squash for dinner).

"Wow!" Kate said. "And how about your basement? Did you tell them why it stinks? That we were making potions?"

"Oh . . . that," Sophie said. She had forgotten about that. Kind of. "I haven't told them about that yet."

"Well, how about your mom's stockings? The ones we played Fashion Show with? Did you tell her Tiptoe didn't rip them and we did?" Kate asked.

"Er . . . no," Sophie said. And she did not really want to. Tiptoe was a kitten. She could not really get in trouble. But Sophie sure could.

Still, if she was really going to be honest, no matter what the consequence was . . .

"I'll tell them," she said to Kate. "I will! I promise!"

From now on, Sophie would be completely, totally honest, just like her new name said.

And to be completely, totally honest, Sophie was getting a little hungry.

She picked up her lunch bag. "I wonder what my mom packed for me," she said.

Then she opened the bag. And right away, she knew.

Someone with a snooty voice from two rows up did, too.

"Ew! Gross!" the voice squealed. It belonged to Mindy VonBoffmann. She spun around and held her nose.

"Quick! Open a window!" Sophie whispered to Kate.

She rolled her lunch bag closed. But it was too late. Mindy's best friend, Lily Lemley, grabbed her nose, too.

"Ew!" Lily cried. "Gross!"

"Who packed egg salad?!" Mindy asked.

Kate looked at Sophie. And Sophie looked at Kate.

Sophie slowly raised her hand. "Um, that was me," she honestly said.

The whole bus started to groan.

"We're here, class!" Ms. Moffly called.

Thank goodness! Sophie thought.

CHAPTER 2

A park ranger met Sophie's class as soon as they got off the bus. Sophie could tell she was a park ranger because of her Smokey Bear hat. That was even before she said, "Hello there! My name is Ranger Fawn."

The ranger's smile was very big. And she was very tall.

"Welcome to Popes Creek," she said, "otherwise known as George Washington's birthplace. Have any of you ever been here before?"

Mindy raised her hand. Of course. She liked to say she had done things (even when she had not).

Most kids shook their heads.

"No. I have not," Sophie honestly said. "My mom wanted to come one time. But my dad said it sounded too boring. And my little brother, Max, won't sit in a stroller anymore. The last time we took him somewhere, he jumped on an old bed and we all got in trouble. So we stayed home and did the Slip 'n Slide instead, because that is never boring, and you're *supposed* to jump on it."

Ranger Fawn looked down at Sophie. "Wow!" she said, smiling. "We have a chatterbox here, don't we?"

Behind her, Toby laughed. Sophie could hear him loud and clear. And Archie. And Mindy. And Lily. And everyone else in their class, she bet.

Sophie wanted to say, "Excuse me. That is not funny. Look at my shirt. I am not a *chatterbox*. I'm Sophie the Honest!"

But Ranger Fawn was already turning around. "Okeydokey, let's get started!" she said.

The ranger led the class down a path along a river. There were shady trees and wooden fences.

Behind one fence were sheep. Behind another were some cows. There were also a bunch of little white buildings and a big house made of brick. But the ranger didn't stop at any of those. Instead, she stopped in front of some lines of white rocks on the ground.

"This is the house where George Washington was born," Ranger Fawn said.

"Huh?" Sophie said. She pointed to the big house made of brick. "Don't you mean *that* house? And by the way, I'm not a chatterbox. I'm just honest," she added.

"Sophie," said Ms. Moffly. She was standing behind the class. "Let's let Ranger Fawn finish talking before we start."

Ranger Fawn smiled a big smile. "That's okay," she said. "I'm *honestly* glad you asked that. In fact, that big house was not George Washington's. It was built later. And it's not exactly what George's house looked like. But it gives you an idea."

Sophie frowned. "Why not just show the real house?" she asked.

15

"Because the real house burned down in 1779," Ranger Fawn explained. She pointed to the white gravel lines on the ground. "All we have of George Washington's first house is this outline that we made."

The other Sophie in the class, Sophie A., spoke up. "Was George Washington okay?"

"Yes, indeed," Ranger Fawn said. "In fact, he didn't even live here when the house burned. By then, he was leading the army in the Revolutionary War. But that wasn't his first job. Does anyone know what that was?"

Mindy was the first to raise her hand. Of course.

"President!" she said.

"Good guess. But no. That came even later. George Washington's first job was *surveying.* Who knows what that is?" Ranger Fawn asked.

Mindy raised her hand again.

"Yes?" Ranger Fawn said.

Mindy opened her mouth. Then she closed it. "Er...I don't know," she said.

"Anyone else?" Ranger Fawn asked.

Sophie spoke up. "I have no idea! But I'm pretty sure my mom just got surveyed on the phone," she said.

Ranger Fawn chuckled. "That's a different kind of surveying. That's when someone asks you questions. The surveying George Washington did was measuring land."

Measuring land? The other kind of surveying sounded like a lot more fun to Sophie, even if her mom made faces during it.

"George Washington taught himself how to survey when he was just fifteen," Ranger Fawn went on. "And one of the first pieces of land he measured was the one you're standing on."

Sophie yawned and leaned over to Kate. "My dad was right. This is boring," she said.

"Excuse me? What did you say?" Ranger Fawn asked, smiling.

Sophie bit her lip. She wanted to say, "Nothing," but she could not. Sophie sighed.

"Um...I said my dad was right. This is boring. Sorry," she added quickly.

"Oh, Sophie," Ms. Moffly said.

Sophie held her breath. She wondered if Ranger Fawn would get mad. But the ranger kept on smiling.

"You know, you're right. There's a lot more fun stuff to see here. Let's move on!" she said.

Ranger Fawn walked ahead, and Sophie's class followed.

Eve skipped up next to Sophie. "Thanks! I didn't want to say anything. But that *was* getting boring," she said.

"Yeah!" Mia agreed.

Sophie grinned at them. "Don't mention it. Just call me Sophie the Honest!"

Ranger Fawn led them down a brick path to one of the small buildings. The doors were big, like barn doors. Sophie and her class went in.

Sophie looked around at all the shelves and benches. There were tools and sawdust everywhere. It was a big mess, if you asked her.

"This looks like my dad's workshop," Sophie said out loud.

The ranger laughed. "Well, it *is* a workshop!" she said. "This is where the blacksmiths and carpenters worked. You see, a farm like this was like a little town. Everything they needed, they had to make themselves."

"Even their TVs?" Dean asked.

Dean liked TV a lot, Sophie knew. He was always talking about some show.

"Well, no," Ranger Fawn said. "Because they didn't have TVs back then."

"Too bad!" Dean said.

What they *did* have were nails and hooks and boxes and buckets and baskets. Ranger Fawn picked them up and showed them to the class.

Then she showed them buildings used for making other stuff, too.

There was a yarn house. That was where wool from the sheep was turned into yarn. It was woven into cloth and made into shirts and pants and coats. Then there was the dairy. That was where milk from the cows was made into cheese and butter. There was even a house just for making apple cider. Sophie liked apple cider a lot. She wished she had a house for that.

"Did you know that George Washington's father had a thousand apple trees?" Ranger Fawn asked the class.

Apple trees! That reminded Sophie of something. She waved her hand in the air, and Ranger Fawn pointed to her.

"No, I did not. But how many *cherry* trees did they have?" Sophie asked.

Ranger Fawn thought for a minute. "None that I know of," she said.

None? Sophie frowned. That did not make sense.

"I mean, before George Washington cut one down," she said.

"Oh, that!" The ranger chuckled. "You're talking about the famous story, aren't you?"

"Yes, I am!" Sophie said.

"Well, I'm afraid that's just a story. We're pretty sure that it's not true," the ranger said.

Huh? Sophie thought.

"What do you mean?" she asked. "Why would someone make up a lie to show that George Washington was honest?"

Ranger Fawn shrugged. "That's a good question."

Thank you, Sophie thought.

"Well, are there any *true* stories that show how honest he was?" she asked.

The ranger rubbed her chin. "Hmmm...not that I can think of," she said. "But that doesn't mean that George wasn't an honest man."

Sophie shook her head, but she stood up straighter. She still could not believe that George Washington had never—ever—cut down a cherry tree. But she bet he would have if he could have. And he would have told his dad, of course.

"So, who wants to see the kitchen now?" Ranger Fawn asked.

Sophie raised her hand. "Not me!" she said. She was getting tired of little buildings. "I'd rather go out to the pasture and pet the sheep. Or can we eat lunch now? I'd really like to do that. I have egg salad. And it's kind of hot. And I don't want it to go bad. One time I ate a tuna sandwich that was bad, and I got really sick. All over the place."

A few kids giggled.

Ranger Fawn looked down at Sophie. "I see," she said. "But all your lunches are in a cooler. So I think they'll be okay. And I know you'll like what we do next. Are there any questions before we move on?" she asked.

Dean raised his hand.

"Yes?" Ranger Fawn said.

"What's your favorite TV show?" Dean asked.

The ranger smiled again. "I really meant are there *history* questions. . . ."

She looked at the class. They all looked back at her and shook their heads.

"No? Then let's go to the kitchen," Ranger Fawn said. Her eyes twinkled as she turned to Dean. "And I really like dancing shows," she added.

CHAPTER 3

Ranger Fawn led Sophie's class down another brick path. They came to another little white house and walked in. It reminded Sophie of something. . . .

But what?

Then it hit her. The Seven Dwarfs' cottage!

Inside was a big table. On it were jugs and wooden bowls. Along one wall was a big fireplace. An orange fire glowed inside.

"Look!" Sophie told Kate. She pointed to a stick broom. "It's just like the one that Snow White used."

"This is George Washington's kitchen," Ranger Fawn told the class. "As you can see, it is in a separate building. Do you know why the kitchen was so far from the main house?"

Sophie bit her lip. Usually, she would have said something like "Because they forgot the kitchen when they built the house?" or "So when George Washington's dad made egg salad, it didn't stink up the house?"

But Sophie had to be honest. So when Ranger Fawn pointed at her, she shook her head. "No, I don't know at all!" she said.

The ranger smiled and pointed to Kate next.

"So when George's babysitter made stuffed cabbage, it didn't stink up the house?" Kate said.

Ranger Fawn laughed. "I don't think George's babysitter made stuffed cabbage. But yes. To keep smells out of the house. That was one reason," she said.

Sophie could not believe it. "I almost said that!" she almost said.

"But there is another reason, too. Can anyone guess?" Ranger Fawn went on.

Sophie raised her hand. Yes. Sure! She could guess.

But Ranger Fawn did not point at her again. She pointed at Mindy instead.

"I know! I know!" Mindy said. "It was so the fire didn't make the house too hot in the summer. Or burn it down."

"Right-o," Ranger Fawn said.

Mindy took a little bow. "I learned that the last time I was here," she said.

Sophie rolled her eyes. She wondered if Mindy was *trying* to make her sick.

"What else do you see that's different from the kitchen in your house?" Ranger Fawn asked the class.

Twenty hands shot up at once. And twenty answers came out in a hurry.

There was no dishwasher. Or fridge. Or stove. Or sink.

There was no microwave for making popcorn. There was no blender for making milk shakes.

All the water came in buckets, from a well outside.

All the cooking was done in the fireplace, in big black pots and pans.

It seemed like a lot of trouble to Sophie.

"Did George Washington's family eat out a lot?" she asked.

Ranger Fawn grinned and shook her head. "Nope," she said. "They made all of their meals right here — including George Washington's favorite breakfast: hoecakes with butter and honey. Hey! Who would like to make George Washington's favorite breakfast right now, right here?"

"Me!" the whole class cheered. And that included Sophie, even though she did not know what a hoecake was. She *did* know that she liked butter and honey!

"Great!" Ranger Fawn said. "Let's split into two

groups. One group will make the hoecakes, and the other group will make the butter."

She moved over to a tall wooden bucket. It had a lid with a hole in the middle and a long pole sticking out of the top.

"Who has used a butter churn before?" Ranger Fawn asked.

Mindy's hand shot up. Of course. So did Lily's. They waved their hands like they were experts. But Sophie was not so sure about that.

Still, it was hard for Sophie to be honest right then. What if the ranger only picked the experts to churn the butter? Sophie really wanted to try it! It was not easy to keep her hand down.

"Okeydokey," Ranger Fawn said. She pointed to Mindy and Lily. "Since you two have done this before, you can make hoecakes. I want to let kids who have not churned butter have a chance."

Mindy's face got pinchy mad. Lily's face did, too. But Sophie was too busy pumping her fist to look at them.

Being honest was awesome!

Ranger Fawn picked Sophie for butter churning. Then—yay!—she picked Kate, too.

Then she picked a bunch of their other friends.

Then she picked Toby and Archie.

Too bad.

Their group gathered around the butter churn. Ranger Fawn poured a big jug of cream into it.

She showed them how to move the stick up and down. That was easy.

Then she told them to have fun and take turns. That was hard.

Grace's mom was in charge of their group. She tried to make it work, but she had never been in charge of Toby and Archie before.

Toby and Archie were very bad at taking turns.

"Me first!" Archie yelled.

"No, me first!" Toby hollered.

They both grabbed the butter churn handle—and they did not let go.

"Boys, boys, boys," Grace's mom said gently.

"Everyone will have a turn. Let your friend go first," she told Toby. "Then you can go."

Sophie shared a look with Kate. Grace's mom did not know Archie and Toby at all!

Toby looked at her and shrugged. He let Archie grab the handle. Then Archie started churning the butter as fast as he could.

"Okay, next," Grace's mom told him.

But Archie did not stop. So Toby grabbed his arms to pull him away. The butter churn rocked....

"Boys!" Grace's mom yelled. She did not sound gentle anymore. "That's it! You're done!"

A few other kids went. Then at last it was Sophie's turn. She couldn't wait! She gripped the handle tightly. And she churned and churned and churned....

Then she stopped.

Boy, were her arms tired! Churning butter was much harder than it looked.

"What's the matter, Sophie? Tired already?" Toby jeered.

Sophie glared at him. She wanted to say no, but she could not lie. She was Sophie the Honest, after all.

"Yes," she muttered. Then she started to stick out her tongue.

But before she could, Ranger Fawn was there.

"The hoecakes are done," she said. "How's the butter coming?"

Sophie wiped her forehead. "I think it's ready," she said.

She stood back and let Ranger Fawn lift the lid. The ranger dipped a scoop into the churn, and Sophie grinned. She could not wait to see the homemade butter!

But what came out did not look like butter. It looked like melted ice cream.

"Aw . . ." Sophie sighed.

So did Kate, and Grace, and some others.

Then Mindy looked over.

"She should have let the experts do it," Mindy said, rolling her eyes.

Not everybody heard Mindy. But Sophie sure

did. She put her hands on her hips. "Mind your own beeswax, Mindy!" she said.

Then she spun around fast. She'd churn that butter and show Mindy! The only thing was... she forgot that the butter churn was right there behind her.

If only the lid had been on it. Then maybe all the white stuff would not have spilled out when Sophie knocked it over. But it did spill out. Everywhere. Even on Ranger Fawn's black boots and Grace's mom's silvery shoes.

Oops.

Sophie had a rule. She did not cry at school. But Sophie was not at school. She was in George Washington's kitchen.

She could feel her throat get tight. Her eyes got hot and leaky.

Then she felt a hand on her shoulder. It was Ranger Fawn's.

"It's okay. Don't worry. Accidents happen," Ranger Fawn told her.

That's the truth! Sophie thought.

She sniffed and felt a little better.

While Grace's mom shook out her shoes, Ranger Fawn got a mop and a bucket. She dried the floor and her boots. Then she poured more cream into a jar.

Everyone took a turn shaking it. By the time they were done, the cream had changed. A lot.

"Is that butter?" Sophie asked.

"Yes, sirree!" said Ranger Fawn.

She set the hoecakes on the table. The other group had made them with cornmeal, water, and salt. They looked a little bit like pancakes. But they did not taste like them at all.

Thank goodness for butter and honey! Sophie thought.

"So, what do you think of the hoecakes?" Ranger Fawn asked the class.

Sophie spoke up. "To be honest, they taste like they came from the workshop."

"Oh, Sophie . . ." Ms. Moffly shook her head.

But Ranger Fawn grinned and nodded. "The truth is, I don't like them much, either. How about we go out to the barn now?" she said. "We can see some animals. Then you guys can have lunch."

"Yay!" the class cheered.

As they walked outside, Kate took Sophie's arm.

"The barn—that reminds me! I have to tell you something *big*, Sophie!" Kate whispered.

Something big?

Sophie looked at her. "What?" she asked at once.

Kate started to speak. Then she looked around and closed her mouth.

"I better tell you in *private*—so no one else hears. After school," she said.

CHAPTER 4

Sophie waited for Kate to tell her the big news. But it was not easy.

Sophie waited through the field trip.

She waited on the bus back to school *and* the bus home.

She waited until she got to Kate's house.

Then she could not wait anymore.

"You have to tell me now!" she cried as they walked into Kate's kitchen. "Honestly! I can't wait anymore!"

"I will, I will. In a second," Kate told her. She

had a giant smile on her face. "Hi, Mrs. Belle! We're home!" she called out.

A cheerful voice called back to them. *"Hellooo! I'll be right there!"*

Mrs. Belle lived in their neighborhood. She had three kids, but they were all grown up. She came over to Kate's in the afternoon and stayed until Kate's mom got home from work.

Kate's mom worked in a doctor's office, but she was not a doctor or a nurse. Sophie was pretty sure her job was to keep people quiet in the waiting room.

Sophie liked Mrs. Belle. She knew a million card games. And she let Sophie and Kate watch TV game shows with her.

She also made stuffed cabbage. It smelled pretty bad. But it actually tasted good.

Mrs. Belle walked into the kitchen. She was wearing her favorite tracksuit. It was bright yellow, like her hair. Sophie knew that it had to be her favorite, since she'd dyed her hair to match.

Mrs. Belle gave Kate and Sophie a hug. "So, how was school today, girls? What did you do?" she asked them.

Kate shrugged. She said the usual: "Okay," and "Not much."

Sophie usually said the same thing. But now that she was Sophie the Honest, "Okay" and "Not much" were not enough.

Sophie took a breath. She cleared her throat.

"To be honest, Mrs. Belle, school was hard today. Before we went on a field trip, we had a spelling quiz first thing. And I thought I knew all the words. But guess what? I studied the words from last week by accident. But then the day got better, because we got to go on our trip. That meant we got to miss meat loaf for lunch. So that was very good. Then I scared Toby and Archie away, and Kate and I got the back seat of the bus. But then I opened my lunch bag. And my mom packed me egg salad. And it stunk up the whole bus. . . ."

Sophie stopped and took another breath. Then she went on.

"Anyway, we walked all over the place where George Washington was born. And I guess we learned some stuff. Stuff like if you ever go on a field trip, do not wear fancy shoes. And that George Washington's teeth probably fell out because he ate hoecakes that tasted like wood. And that he did not have a TV. But even if he did, I bet it would have gotten burned. And that even presidents can have the most boring jobs in the world."

Mrs. Belle's eyes were wide. She looked surprised. So did Kate.

"My goodness! Sophie, you're a little chatterbox today!" Mrs. Belle exclaimed.

Chatterbox? *Again?*

Sophie stood up very straight. She proudly raised her chin.

"I'm just being *honest*, Mrs. Belle. From now on, that is who I am," Sophie said. She tugged on her shirt so her *H* showed better. "Sophie the Honest, at your service!"

"I see! So tell me, and be *honest!* What can I get you girls to eat?" Mrs. Belle said.

That was when Kate spoke up. "Cookies, please!"

Mrs. Belle got out a box of cookies with fudge stripes on top. She poured two cups of milk and let the girls squeeze chocolate into them.

"Whoa!" Mrs. Belle said. "I think that's enough."

Sophie stopped squeezing and licked her fingers. Then she remembered what she had been waiting for all day.

"Kate! You have to tell me your big news!" she said.

"Oh, right!" Kate said. She took a sip of chocolate milk and grinned. "But first, do I have a mustache?"

Sophie rolled her eyes. "Yes," she said. She sipped her milk so she had one, too. "Now go on!" she told Kate.

Kate turned to Mrs. Belle. "Mrs. Belle, tell Sophie about your daughter!"

Mrs. Belle winked. "Well, she's moved back to town. Finally!" she told Sophie.

"Oh...," Sophie said. She guessed that was exciting...for Mrs. Belle.

Kate leaned over. "That's not all," she said.

Then Mrs. Belle told Sophie that her daughter had bought a horse farm.

"Oh," Sophie said. That was more exciting.

Then Mrs. Belle told Sophie that her daughter had invited Kate to come ride horses. And that Kate could bring two friends. And sleep over. *And* they could do it all that weekend!

"Oh!" Sophie said. That was not just exciting... it was the most fantastic, amazing, awesome thing ever, in the whole world!

"Have you ever ridden a horse before?" Mrs. Belle asked.

"No. Never." Sophie shook her head. "But it has always been my lifelong dream," she said very seriously.

Kate looked at her funny. "It has?"

"Yes, honest!" Sophie said. "I just didn't know it until now."

Then Sophie looked at Kate. And Kate looked at Sophie.

"Are you thinking what I'm thinking?" Kate asked.

"I think so!" Sophie said.

They gulped down their milk and each grabbed a handful of cookies.

"Thanks a lot, Mrs. Belle!" they said. "We have to go outside and practice!"

Sophie and Kate ran straight to Kate's swing set. They straddled the swings like they were horses. They grabbed the chains and rocked and yelled, "Giddyup!" as loudly as they could.

"Whoa!" Kate said at last. She patted the air where her horse's head would be. "Easy now, Lightning. Not too fast."

Sophie pretended to pat her horse, too. "Good girl, Buttercup. Nice jumping!" she told her.

Then Sophie suddenly thought of something. Something that made her horse stop. Was *pretending* to ride a horse *honest*?

"What's wrong, Sophie?" Kate asked. "You look like your horse threw you off."

Sophie sighed. She swung her leg over the swing so that she was facing forward.

"What's wrong is that I forgot to be honest. No more pretending for me," Sophie said.

"Huh?" Kate said. "But we *like* pretending."

"I know. But pretending isn't honest," Sophie said. "At least, I don't think so."

Sophie sighed again. This time, Kate sighed with her.

They were both quiet for a minute.

"Can *I* still pretend?" Kate asked.

Sophie nodded. "Sure. Why not?"

Kate started to gallop on her horse. Then she stopped. "It's not the same by myself."

"Sorry," Sophie said glumly. She didn't want to ruin Kate's fun, but she had to be true to her new name!

"That's okay," Kate said. "The only problem is that we pretend a lot."

They were both quiet again.

"I know! Let's talk instead," Sophie said, swinging back and forth. "Tell me. Who else are you going to ask to come to the horse farm?"

Sophie knew that was a tough question, since Kate could only bring two friends. Sophie was Kate's number one best friend. But there was a four-way tie for number two. Grace and Sydney sat at their table in room 10. And Eve and Mia played the most with them at recess.

Kate shrugged. "Grace is nice," she said. "But she can be a little bossy. And Eve and Mia are fun. But Eve still can't sleep over. She always has to call her mom. And Mia laughs really, really loud. She could scare the horses. So I guess I'll ask Sydney. What do you think?" Kate asked.

Sophie nodded. "I think that sounds good," she said honestly.

Then Kate chewed her hair. Sophie knew she did that when she was nervous.

"But what if Grace and Eve and Mia find out?" Kate went on. "I don't want them to be mad. Or feel bad."

Sophie waved her hand.

"Don't worry," she told Kate. "Sydney is good at keeping secrets. How could anyone find out?"

CHAPTER 5

Sophie could not wait to get home and tell her mom the big news.

But her mom asked her a question first: "Sophie, how was school?"

Sophie had to be honest!

By the time Sophie got to the butter-churning part, her mom had to stop her.

"I'm sorry, Sophie," her mom said. "I want to hear more. I really do. But you're such a chatterbox today. And I have so much to do."

Chatterbox! *Again?*

Sophie was just trying to be honest! Why did

47

grown-ups ask questions if they didn't want to hear the truth?

Still, honestly, she was glad to stop talking about her day. She spotted Tiptoe, her kitten, near her feet. She bent down and scooped her up. Then she tickled Tiptoe's chin. Tiptoe liked that, Sophie knew.

Sophie looked at the stove. A pot of red sauce was bubbling. It smelled very, very yummy. "What are you making, Mom?"

"Lasagna. Dad's favorite. I want to surprise him," her mom said.

"Can I help?" Sophie asked.

Her mom smiled but shook her head. "I'm sorry, but I have to do this fast so I can clean the house," she said. "Aunt Maggie called. She invited herself over for dinner. Again."

Sophie's mom's smile was gone. She looked at the clock and let out a groan. "What is Aunt Maggie's problem?" she asked.

Sophie shrugged and told the truth: "I do not know."

Sophie's mom smiled again. "I don't, either. I just hope she doesn't bring any more junk with her. If only she knew we throw most of it out," she said, shaking her head.

Brring-brring-brring!

"Could you answer the phone, Sophie?" her mom asked. Her hands were covered with cheese. "If it's for me, just say I'm not here, please."

Sophie ran for the phone. She was happy to get it. Almost always, her mom or her dad or her older sister, Hayley, answered it first.

Sophie punched the "talk" button. "Hello?"

"Hello!" said a very loud voice on the other end. "Aunt Maggie here! Who is this?"

"Hi, Aunt Maggie. This is Sophie." She cleared her throat. "Sophie the Honest!"

She couldn't help smiling. What a good name she had picked!

"Sophie the *who*?" said Aunt Maggie. "Sophie the *Olive*?"

Sometimes Sophie forgot that Aunt Maggie didn't hear well.

"No, Aunt Maggie." Sophie sighed. "It's just me. Sophie," she said.

She would wait until Aunt Maggie got there to make her new name clear.

"Ah, Sophie. How are you, dear?" Aunt Maggie asked.

"Well . . . ," Sophie began.

"That's nice, dear," said Aunt Maggie. "Is your mother there?"

Sophie thought about that for a second.

"Yes," she said finally. "And no."

"What's that?" said Aunt Maggie. "I'm sorry, dear. I didn't get that. Was that a yes? Or a no?"

"Both," Sophie said, as loudly as she could, into the phone. "Yes, because my mom is here. And no, because she told me to say she's not. But I can't lie. Because I am honest!"

Sophie turned to smile at her mom. Her mom did not smile back.

Oops.

"Um, I don't think you want to talk to my mom, anyway," Sophie went on. "She looks a little mad.

And her hands are in the lasagna. And the house is a big mess. And she still has to clean it before you get here. And —"

Just then, Sophie's mom took the phone.

"Are you going to ask Aunt Maggie what her problem is?" Sophie asked.

Quickly, Sophie's mom put her hand over the phone. "Why don't you go do your homework, Sophie?" she said.

"Do I have to?" Sophie asked. Honestly, she did not want to. Her homework was a word find. Those were almost as boring as surveying.

"Yes!" her mom said.

Sophie sighed. She headed to her room. On the way, her sister, Hayley, stopped her. She was in the playroom with Max, their little brother.

Hayley was in fifth grade. But she acted like she was grown up.

Max was two. And he acted like that, pretty much.

Just then, he was running a toy front loader over Hayley's foot.

"Sophie! There you are! I've been waiting for you. Mom asked me to watch Max for her. But now it's your turn," Hayley said.

Sophie shrugged. "I can't," she said. She was happy to be honest this time! "Mom told me to do my homework."

Hayley rolled her eyes. "You can do both, like I did," she said. "I have to call Sam right now and ask him what to do for homework."

Sophie frowned. She was confused. She knew who Sam was. He was Dean's big brother. And he was the boy Hayley *like*-liked.

Sophie knew this because Hayley wrote Sam's name all over her notebooks. And she tried to walk by him all the time in school.

"But you just said you already did your homework," Sophie said.

Hayley made a face. "That's not *really* why I'm calling him," she said. And with that, she lifted Max's truck off her foot and left the room.

Sophie sat down and tried to do her word find. But doing homework with Max was hard.

It was not because he talked a lot. In fact, he did not talk at all. (Which was weird, Sophie thought.) But he made a lot of other noises. Noises like *BANG!* and *CRASH!* and *BOOM!* and *WHOMP!*

Sophie was glad when she finally heard another sound.

BEEP-BEEP! Aunt Maggie's car horn!

"Come on, Max," Sophie said. "Aunt Maggie's here. Let's see what she brought."

Sophie's Great-aunt Maggie never came empty-handed. She always came with stuff. It was all stuff from her big, old house. And it was all stuff that Sophie's mom called junk.

That day, she had two bags when she walked in the door. Sophie could see them under her shawl. The shawl was as big as Sophie's bedspread. Aunt Maggie always wore it instead of a coat.

Aunt Maggie set down the bags. "Hello, darling children!" She wrapped Sophie and Max up in a hug in her shawl.

Her shawl smelled a lot like perfume. And a little like wet dog.

Then Aunt Maggie reached into a bag and pulled out a glass bowl. It was full of matchbooks.

Wow! Sophie hoped it was for her. She had never had matches before!

But Aunt Maggie handed it to Max.

"Maximilian, dear! Look what I have for you!" she said.

Sophie stepped back. Matches? And a glass bowl? For Max? She did not think that was a very good idea.

Max reached up to grab the bowl, but Sophie's mom swooped in.

"Maybe *I* should take that, Aunt Maggie," she said.

Aunt Maggie grinned and nodded. "If you like it that much, it's yours!" she said.

Then she pulled out a plant. It looked pretty dead.

"Here, Maxy. Give this a little water. It will grow like wild," Aunt Maggie said.

Max grabbed it happily and dumped it onto the

floor. He sat down in the dirt. Then he scooped some up and ate it.

Sophie looked at her mom. She had put the glass bowl on a table. Now her head was in her hands.

Aunt Maggie was already reaching back into her bags. Two more things came out.

One was a big book. It looked old and had two words, "LATIN GRAMMAR," on the cover.

The other was a pin. It was shaped like a big bug. And it was covered, almost, with jewels. (Some had fallen off the bottom.)

Still, it was the best thing Aunt Maggie had ever brought, by far!

Sophie was glad she had not gotten the matches. She wanted the bug pin very, very much.

But Aunt Maggie handed the book to Sophie.

"Sophie-Olive, darling, what do you think?" she asked.

Sophie thought hard for a minute. She was Sophie the Honest. She had to tell the truth.

"I think...I would like that bug pin a lot more," Sophie said.

Sophie hoped Aunt Maggie's feelings were not hurt. But Aunt Maggie didn't look hurt. She looked like she hadn't heard Sophie.

"What's that?" she asked with one hand behind her ear.

"I said, I think I would like that bug pin!" Sophie said again, a little more loudly.

"You mean this *broach*?" said Aunt Maggie.

Broach? Was that like a roach? Sophie wondered.

"I guess so," Sophie said. "But it looks like a ladybug to me."

Aunt Maggie smiled. "Well, if there's one thing I like, it's a girl who's honest. It's yours!" she said.

She pinned the broach to Sophie's shirt.

"Thank you!" Sophie said. She felt as sparkly as the ladybug...or broach...or whatever.

"I guess I'll be giving this book to Hayley," said Aunt Maggie. "I wonder where she is...."

She shrugged and put the book down. Then she pulled out something else. It was orange and shaped like a pumpkin. Sophie was pretty sure it was a lamp. And she was very sure it was broken.

Aunt Maggie gave it a pat. "This is for your dad. He can fix it up. It will be fun! I hate to throw things out, don't you?" she said.

Sophie looked up from her pin.

"Oh, we like to throw stuff out," she told Aunt Maggie. "Mom throws out most of the stuff you give us. And my dad can't fix anything. And Hayley is in her room. She's trying to get a boyfriend by telling him lies about her homework."

"Sophie!" her mom said. She was shaking her head.

"Sophie!" said Hayley. She had just walked in. Why did everyone look so mad?

"Aunt Maggie!" said Sophie's dad. He had just walked in, too. "I didn't know you were coming. This is a surprise! And mmm...smells good! What's for dinner?" he asked.

"Don't ask, Dad," Sophie told him. "It's lasagna. And it's a surprise, too."

CHAPTER 6

By the next day, Sophie had learned a lot about being honest.

In some ways it was easy—hear a question, say the truth. But in some ways it was hard. Sometimes some people did not want to hear the truth.

And sometimes some people, like Aunt Maggie, could not hear the truth (or anything else, really).

Still, Sophie had a name, and she had to live up to it. She was Sophie the Honest!

Or was she?

When Sophie got to school the next day, that was

not what she was called. Not at all. No, everyone was calling her Sophie the Chatterbox!

It happened almost as soon as she walked into the classroom.

"Good morning, Sophie," said Ms. Moffly. "What a pretty ladybug pin. Where did it come from?"

Sophie grinned.

"Actually, Ms. Moffly, this is a *broach*. And it came from my Aunt Maggie. She invited herself over yesterday. She likes to do that a lot. And she likes to bring us junk, like the can opener she gave me last time. But this is much better. And much, much better than —"

Just then, Toby walked by. His hands were clapped over his ears.

"Look out! Chatterbox alert!" he called.

Of course, Archie had to say something, too.

"Help, she's still a chatterbox! We're doomed!" he yelled.

Sophie glared at them both. Honestly, they were the worst!

"Boys!" said Ms. Moffly. "That is quite enough. There will be no name-calling in this classroom."

Unless it's a really great name...like Sophie the Honest, Sophie thought.

Then Ms. Moffly turned back to Sophie. "Well, Sophie, I like your *broach* very much. And I would love to hear more about it. But it's time for class to start."

Ms. Moffly reached for the light switch. She flashed the lights three times.

"Has everyone put their homework in the basket?" she asked the class.

There were a few nods. Some "Not yet"s. A few "Yeah"s. And one "Mine was the first." That was Mindy. Of course.

Sophie sighed. Oh, yeah. Her homework. She had kind of hoped that Ms. Moffly would forget about that.

She raised her hand slowly. "I don't have my homework, Ms. Moffly," she said.

"Oh? Why not?" Ms. Moffly asked.

Sophie sighed a big, loud sigh. "My brother ate it."

Right away, the whole class started laughing... but Ms. Moffly didn't. She frowned.

"Your brother *ate* it? I find that very hard to believe, Sophie," she said.

What? Her? Hard to believe? But she was Sophie the Honest!

"It's true!" Sophie said, talking faster and faster. "Honest! I started to do the homework. But then Aunt Maggie showed up and I had to stop. When I went back to get it, it was all chewed up and on the floor. And it had to be my brother who did it. We don't have a dog. Just a kitten. And she never eats paper. But she does eat plants. And Jell-O. Once."

Sophie took a gulp of air.

"You have to believe me, Ms. Moffly. You have to!" she finished.

Ms. Moffly's frown went away. A calm smile took its place.

"I do believe you, Sophie. You can do another word find tonight," she said.

☆ ☆ ☆

"That was close," Sophie told Kate a little while later. They were walking around the classroom, *surveying* it with a measuring tape—just like they'd learned about at George Washington's house.

Kate held her measuring tape up to Sophie's bug broach. "What was close?" she asked.

"When Ms. Moffly thought that I was lying," said Sophie. "Can you believe it? Me? I'm Sophie the Honest!"

"Oh, right!" Kate nodded.

"And what about all this 'chatterbox' stuff?" Sophie went on. "Honestly, that has to stop."

"Well . . ." Kate shrugged. She held her measuring tape up to a ruler. "Twelve inches. Exactly." Then she looked at Sophie. "Maybe you're both."

Sophie had to frown. *Both?* She didn't think so.

"But I'm not a chatterbox!" she protested. "I'm honest. I tell the truth, the whole truth, and nothing but the truth. That's all."

"I know. But maybe you could tell the whole truth without talking so much," Kate said.

Sophie thought about that for a second. It was a pretty good idea. She was getting tired of talking so much, anyway.

"I'll see what I can do," she said.

With that, she took one end of the measuring tape. Kate stretched it across their table.

"Four feet," Kate said.

Then Sophie pointed to Sydney's empty chair.

"Have you asked Sydney about riding horses this weekend yet?" she asked.

Kate shook her head. "Not yet," she said. "I think I will after school." She put her thumb and finger together and pulled them like a zipper across her lips. "Remember," she said, "this is a secret."

Sophie zipped her lips back. "Got it!"

Just then, Dean walked up with his measuring

tape. He said he wanted to ask Sophie something. And he wanted an honest answer.

"You've come to the right girl!" Sophie said. Yes! Her name was working!

"I was just wondering. How come your sister calls my brother about homework every night?" Dean asked.

Sophie cleared her throat. She could answer this question, no problem. And she did not need to be a chatterbox to do it!

"Because my sister has a great big crush on him," she said simply.

Dean nodded. "I knew it. I saw the same thing happen on TV."

As he walked away, Sophie grinned. "You're welcome, Dean!" she called after him. Then she turned to Kate. "Better?"

Kate nodded. "Much."

Sophie was ready for her next question. But it did not come right away. Instead, it came just before lunch. She and Grace were at the classroom sink, washing their hands.

"I hope your mom's shoes are okay," Sophie said. She still felt a little bad when she thought about spilling the butter.

"They're not. But it's fine," Grace told her. "My mom is happy. Now she has a reason to buy new ones. Pass me the soap. Oh, and guess what!"

"What?" asked Sophie.

"We set up our trampoline in the backyard," Grace said. "Want to come over this weekend and jump?"

A trampoline! Sophie loved those!

She was all ready to say, "Yes!" But then she remembered Kate and the horses.

"Yes. I do want to. But I can't," she said carefully.

"Aw, too bad. Why not?" Grace asked.

Why not?

"Um . . ." Sophie froze.

She wished she could say, "Oh, no reason." Or "Because my sister has a very important ballet recital. And I don't want to go. They're always so boring. But I *have* to."

She was Sophie the Honest. She couldn't say those things. But maybe she could change the subject.

Sophie pulled her hands out from under the water. "Paper towel, please?" she asked.

Grace tore one off and passed it.

"Thank you," Sophie said. *That was easy!* she thought, grinning.

"So what are you doing this weekend? Tell me!" Grace said.

Oh, no.

Sophie crumpled her paper towel. She thought of Kate zipping her lips. But Sophie had to tell the truth. She couldn't be Sophie the Honest if she lied!

She took a deep breath.

"I'm doing something with Kate," she said.

"What?" Grace asked.

"Um... riding horses...," Sophie mumbled. "Boy, am I hungry! Aren't you?" she asked.

"That sounds fun!" Grace said. "Where are you riding horses?"

"Um..." Sophie looked up at the clock. Why wasn't it time for lunch yet? "Kate's babysitter, Mrs. Belle...her daughter has a horse farm...and we're going there...and sleeping over...," she said.

Grace smiled a very big smile. "Wow! Can I come, too?" she asked.

Sophie bit her lip. She was feeling hot. "Um, no. You can't."

Now Grace frowned a very big frown. She crossed her arms. "Why not?" she asked.

Sophie took another deep breath. "I'm sorry. I can't tell you," she said.

Then she turned around. But Grace turned with her. Her hands were on her hips.

"I thought you were Sophie the *Honest.* Or are you just a chatterbox?" Grace said.

"I am not a chatterbox!" Sophie said.

She was Sophie the Honest! But then she thought about what that meant. It meant telling the truth...no matter what the consequences were.

"Okay," Sophie said, standing up straight and tall. "The truth is, Kate can only invite two friends. And she's inviting me and Sydney. She would have picked you, Grace. But you are too bossy sometimes. But don't feel bad. Mia laughs too loud. And Eve gets scared at sleepovers."

"Bossy?" Grace repeated when Sophie stopped for air.

Then Ms. Moffly flashed the lights. It was time for lunch. At last!

☆　　☆　　☆

Some days, Sophie liked school lunch. Like pizza days—those were good. And some days, she did not. Like this day. Chili day. Blech!

"No, thank you," she told the lunch lady when she offered Sophie a scoop of chili. "To be honest, it reminds me of mud." Sophie took two rolls instead. And four pats of butter.

Then she turned to see Kate in line behind her. Kate did not look happy at all.

"I know," Sophie said. "Chili. Blech!"

But Kate didn't nod or smile. What she did do was shout, "How could you, Sophie?!"

Then she turned and stomped off.

CHAPTER 7

*H*ow could she?

How could she *what*?

How could she take two rolls? But she had done that before.

How could she take four butters? Okay. Maybe that was too much.

Or how could she have gotten into the lunch line without Kate? Maybe that was it. Sophie should have waited. But Kate had gone to the bathroom, so Sophie thought it was okay.

She paid for her lunch, grabbed her tray, and hurried to catch up with Kate. Sophie wasn't sure where Kate was going. She didn't even have her lunch yet.

"I'm sorry! Honest! I'll wait for you next time. I promise!" she said.

But Kate didn't look any happier. In fact, she looked even more mad. "That's not what I'm mad about," she said.

"Then what is it?" Sophie asked.

"I'm mad because you told everyone about my horse-riding sleepover!" Kate cried. "And now they're all mad at me!"

Oh.

Sophie felt like her feet were starting to sink into the floor.

"I'm sorry, Kate. Really, really sorry! But I didn't tell everyone!" Sophie crossed her heart. "Honest!"

Kate gave her a look. It was a look she gave to Toby sometimes. "Don't lie!" she said.

"I'm not lying," said Sophie. "I only told Grace. But I had to. She made me."

"How did she make you?" Kate asked, putting her hands on her hips.

"Well . . . she asked me," Sophie said.

Kate shook her head. "And did she make you tell her I said she was bossy? And that Mia laughs too loud? And that Eve gets scared?" Kate asked. "Because that's what they said!"

Oh, no!

Grace isn't just bossy, thought Sophie. *She's bad at keeping secrets, too!*

"I didn't want to tell Grace all of that. I just had to," Sophie said to Kate. "I was being honest. That's who I am! Remember?"

Sophie smiled at Kate. She had to understand. She just had to!

But Kate did not smile back. She crossed her arms instead.

"You know what?" Kate said. "Your name shouldn't be Sophie the Honest. And it shouldn't be Sophie the Chatterbox, either." She glared so hard at Sophie, Sophie had to look away. "It should be Sophie the Big Mouth, if you ask me!"

Ouch! Kate's words hurt more than any pinch from Toby ever had.

"I'm sorry, Kate," said Sophie, looking down at her shoes. "Don't be mad. I'm your best friend."

Kate shook her head slowly. "*Honestly*, Sophie, I don't think you are. I just can't trust you."

And with that, Kate walked off to get her own rolls and butter.

Sophie looked around. One whole lunch table was staring at her. But Sophie felt so bad, she didn't even care.

☆　　☆　　☆

It was Sophie's worst lunch. Ever. Worse than the one where she dropped the meatball sandwich in her lap.

For one thing, there was no one to sit with.

Not Kate, of course. She was too mad. She sat with Sydney.

And not Grace or Eve or Mia. They were too mad to sit with Sophie *or* Kate.

Plus Grace had told more girls about Kate's horse-riding party. And now they were mad, too.

That left only the boys to sit with. But who wanted to sit with them?

Toby walked up to Sophie as she sat all alone. "Why aren't you sitting with Kate, Chatterbox?" he asked.

Sophie wanted to say, "Mind your own beeswax!" But she was Sophie the Honest. She had to tell the truth...even to Toby.

She lifted her chin. "Because I don't think we're friends anymore," she said.

She was glad that Toby kept on walking. She was pretty sure that if he had stayed, her "no crying in school" rule would have been broken.

Sophie picked up a roll off her tray.

It had raisins in it. Gross!

☆　　☆　　☆

The rest of the day went by slowly. (And staying inside for recess—Sophie's consequence from yesterday—didn't help.)

Finally, it was three o'clock. But for Sophie, that just meant sitting by herself on the bus home.

Or even worse, sitting next to Ella.

Ella Fitzgibbon was in kindergarten. She lived next door to Sophie. She had always been a pest. But then Sophie had saved her life. She'd stopped Ella from running into the street in front of a car, and had become Ella's hero. Since then, Ella had been worse than ever!

"Sophie!" Ella squeaked. She pointed to the empty seat next to Sophie. "Is Kate sitting here?"

Sophie looked across the bus. Kate was in a seat already. She had to be honest. "No."

"Oh, goody!" Ella said. She plopped down.

She smelled like crayons and glue and . . . rotten fruit? Sophie sniffed. What *was* that?

"Ooh! I like your bug pin!" Ella said. "Hey! Want to see my shrunken head?"

Before Sophie could say yes or no, Ella held up something small and wrinkly. "I made it with an apple! Do you like it?" she asked.

Sophie looked at it closely. It was shrunken, yeah. But a head? Sophie didn't think so.

She sighed and turned to the window. Suddenly, a hand was on Sophie's shoulder. Someone was leaning over the seat.

Kate? Sophie looked up hopefully. Did Kate want to talk to her again?

No.

It was just Sophie's big sister, Hayley.

"How could you?!" she cried.

CHAPTER 8

*H*ow could she?

How could she what *this* time?

"How could you tell Sam that I had a crush on him?" Hayley whispered.

Sophie sat back in her seat. She had not known that a whisper could sound so mad.

"But I didn't!" Sophie said quickly. She had never even talked to Sam!

"Then how did he find out?" asked Hayley.

"I don't know." Sophie shrugged. "Maybe Dean told him."

Oops.

Sophie should have stopped, maybe, after "I don't know."

"Did you tell *Dean*?!" Hayley asked her.

Sophie tried to swallow the lump in her throat. Two times. But it did not work.

"Yes. I did. But I had to. He asked me," Sophie said.

Hayley flipped her long hair over one shoulder. "Thanks a lot for ruining my life, Sophie!" she cried, storming off to sit with her best friend, Kim.

"What was that about?" Ella asked, nibbling on her apple.

Sophie sighed and rubbed her eyes. "That was about being honest," she said. "And don't eat your shrunken head, Ella. That's disgusting!"

☆   ☆   ☆

Sophie's bus ride home took fifteen whole minutes. That gave her a lot of time to think about things.

Things like:

If honesty was the best policy, why had everything turned out so bad?

And why did Kate have to ignore her?

And why did Hayley have to give her dirty looks?

And why did Ella have to ask so many questions?

By the time the bus got to Sophie's stop, she was tired of thinking...and very tired of having to answer Ella's questions with the truth.

Questions like:

"Why is Kate sitting all the way over there?"

And "Why is she mad at you?"

And "Why did you tell everybody something Kate didn't want you to?"

And "If Kate's not talking to you, are you free to play after school?"

And "Yay! Should we play at my house or yours?"

But what could she do? Sophie the Honest had to tell the truth.

"I guess we should play at your house," Sophie told Ella.

Hayley was so mad. Ella's house would be safer, Sophie was pretty sure of that.

☆　　☆　　☆

It had been a long time since Sophie had been to Ella's house. Mostly because Sophie had made up good excuses not to go.

That didn't keep Ella from coming over to Sophie's house. But it *did* keep Sophie from having to play Stuffed Animal Beauty Salon in Ella's bubble-gum pink room. Or worse, Sleeping Beauty. That had been Ella's favorite game for months, ever since she had seen the movie.

When they reached Ella's house, Ella opened the back door. "Mom-my!" she called. "I'm home! I have a shrunken head! And Sophie!"

"What a treat," Ella's mom called back. "I'll be there in a sec!"

Ella took Sophie's hand and dragged her into the kitchen.

A second later, Mrs. Fitzgibbon walked—no, *waddled*—into the room.

"Sophie, how nice to see you!" she said. "My, you have grown!"

Sophie stared. She could not help it. "So have you, Mrs. Fitzgibbon!" she said. It was the truth.

Ella's mom grabbed her round middle and laughed. Ella laughed, too.

"She's having a baby, silly!" said Ella.

Oh!

"So, are you girls hungry?" Mrs. Fitzgibbon asked.

"Yes!" Ella answered.

Sophie said yes, too. But she knew what saying yes meant. It meant vegetables for snack. That was another reason Sophie did not love visiting Ella's house.

Sophie was glad that Ella's mom had not asked, "How was school?" That was not an honest answer she wanted to give.

Mrs. Fitzgibbon filled a plate with green stuff, and Sophie reached for a celery stick.

"Ah-ah-ah!" Ella's mom wagged her finger. "Have you washed your hands yet?" she asked.

Sophie almost said yes. That was what she wanted to do. But she still had to be honest, so she shook her head and said no. Then she went to the sink and washed up.

"Girls, why don't you go play now?" Mrs. Fitzgibbon said after their snack. She held up Ella's shrunken apple. "I'll find a place to hang this precious little head!"

Ella grabbed Sophie by the hand. But Sophie knew how to find Ella's room all on her own. It was the one so pink that it glowed.

Inside, Ella dove for a pile of dress-up clothes. She chose a pink dress and put it on. Then she gave Sophie a sword, a witch hat, and a magic wand.

"Let's play Sleeping Beauty!" Ella said. "I'll be Sleeping Beauty. And you pretend to be everyone else. Okay?"

Sophie put down the sword and the witch hat.

(She kind of liked the magic wand.) Then she looked at Ella.

"No, it's not okay. I want to play something else," Sophie said very honestly. "And besides, I can't pretend."

Ella looked confused. "Why not?" she asked.

Sophie crossed her arms. "Pretending is not honest," she said.

"Oh," Ella said. She was quiet for a minute. "Okay." She brightened up. "Let's play Stuffed Animal Beauty Salon instead!"

"Sorry." Sophie shook her head. "That's pretending also."

Ella's chin started to tremble. "But there's nothing else to do!" she cried.

A second later, she was sobbing. Stuff started to leak out of her nose.

"Okay! Okay! I'll pretend!" Sophie told her.

Ella sniffed. She looked up at Sophie. Her eyes were dry. Her chin was still.

"Really?" she said. "Goody! I'm Sleeping Beauty. You're the witch."

Sophie sighed and nodded. She knew the drill.

Ella pricked her finger. Then she fell to the floor.

After a minute, Sophie nudged her.

Yep. Ella was really asleep. Same thing every time.

Sophie plopped down on Ella's pink bedspread. She found a stuffed horse and hugged it tight. She tried to think about something, anything else. Like Tiptoe. Or even her homework.

But it wasn't any use. All she could think about was Kate.

CHAPTER 9

Sophie hoped the next day would be better. But it was even worse.

Kate ignored her at the bus stop. And again on the bus to school. And in their classroom, too.

That was even after Ms. Moffly asked, "Who has something they'd like to talk about this morning?"

And after Sophie raised her hand and said the truth: "I do."

And after Toby snickered and said, "Chatterbox! Of course you do!"

And after Sophie stuck her tongue out at him. Two times.

Then she took a deep breath. "I want to talk about how just because I am honest does not mean I am a bad person," she said. "And how I am a good friend. Really. And how I am very, very sorry if I hurt anyone's feelings. Oh. And how I am not a chatterbox. Honest! That is all. Thank you."

Then Mindy raised her hand and said, "How come Sophie gets to talk about herself, Ms. Moffly? The last time I wanted to talk about myself, you said no."

And Lily said, "That's a good question."

And Mia said, "Because you already talked about yourself for five days in a row, Mindy."

And Mindy said, "That's not true!"

And Lily said, "Mindy's right. That's not true. It was four days. At the most."

And Archie said, "I want to talk about *me*! I just learned how to burp the national anthem!"

And Dean said, "I want to talk about this show I saw last night. It was awesome."

And Ms. Moffly said, "You know what, class? I think it's time to get to work."

But Sophie did not hear any of that. She only heard one thing. It was Kate muttering, "Whatever."

Ouch! It felt like something was poking Sophie's heart. She looked down to see if it was her broach. It was not.

"Remember your rule," she told herself. "No crying in school. No matter what."

But the truth was it was hard not to. Sophie missed Kate so much.

She missed Kate when the class watched a movie about the metric system. Sophie and Kate usually braided each other's hair during movies. Especially during boring ones like that. But Kate kept every centimeter of her hair to herself.

Sophie missed Kate in gym when they played Partner Is Always It.

"Find a partner!" Mr. Hurley, the gym teacher, hollered.

Sophie looked around. She wasn't used to picking a partner. She and Kate were always a pair.

Ben was standing next to her. He was the nicest boy in her class. She turned to him and sighed.

"Want to be my partner?" she asked.

"Sure, Sophie," he said. "But I should warn you —"

Just then, Mr. Hurley blew his whistle and hollered, "Begin!"

Sophie started to run. "Go, go, go!" she shouted to Ben.

The object of the game was easy: Tag everyone who was not your partner. If you got tagged, you had to sit down. Only your partner could free you by tagging you again.

If both partners got tagged, there was only one way to free each other. You had to look around until you saw each other. Then you both had to give a thumbs-up.

Sophie saw Ben get tagged. But Toby tagged her before she could free him.

She sat down and waved...and waved...and waved...and waved to Ben.

Then Sophie noticed something. Ben wasn't wearing his glasses.

Sophie sighed. He couldn't see her, so they couldn't give each other the thumbs-up! She watched the other kids run around. And she sat for the rest of the half hour.

Then it was time for lunch. Sophie knew she would miss Kate then. And she did.

She even missed Kate back in their classroom. And they were sitting next to each other!

"Sydney, would you please ask Sophie to pass the blue pencil?" Kate said.

They were sitting at their table, using their measurements to make maps of the classroom. This was something surveyors like George Washington did, too.

"Huh?" Sydney looked up at Kate. "Why don't you ask her?"

"Because I'm not talking to Sophie," Kate said simply.

"Oh." Sydney nodded. She shared a look with Grace. "Um, Sophie, Kate says to pass the blue pencil."

Sophie looked down at the blue pencil in her hand. She honestly couldn't stand having Kate mad at her like this!

"Tell Kate that if she wants it so bad, she should ask me herself," Sophie said.

Sydney sighed and turned back to Kate. "Sophie says if you want it so bad, you should ask her yourself."

Kate rolled her eyes. Then she took a green pencil from the basket.

"Never mind. I don't need it. Tell Sophie to keep it," Kate said.

Sydney nodded and looked at Sophie. "Kate said never mind. You can kee —"

Sophie threw her pencil into the basket.

"I heard her!" she said.

☆　　☆　　☆

$\mathcal{B}$y the end of the day, Sophie was sure of one thing. This had been the worst day of her whole life. All eight years!

Sophie wished she could call her mom to come and pick her up. Then at least she wouldn't have to ride the bus home again. Sophie wasn't sure what was worse: Kate not talking to her for the whole bus ride, or Ella talking too much.

And then there was Hayley. She was already on the bus when Sophie climbed aboard. Sophie tried to sneak by, but Hayley spotted her.

She pointed to Sophie.

"You!" she cried.

Sophie sighed. Not again!

Sophie wished she could get off the bus. But it was too late. There was a whole line of kids behind her.

"Find a seat! Keep it moving!" Mrs. Blatt, the bus driver, called out.

Sophie plopped down in the seat across from Hayley. She cleared her throat once. Then she cleared it again.

"Look, Hayley, I know I ruined your life. And I am really, really sorry. But if it makes you feel better, my life is ruined, too," Sophie said, looking down at her hands.

Then Ella's head popped up. She had crawled under the seats to Sophie. She wiggled and pulled herself up.

"Hi, Sophie! I found you," she said.

Great.

Sophie slumped down in her seat and held her head.

"What's wrong?" Ella asked.

"Yeah, what's wrong, Sophie? Who said you ruined my life?" Hayley asked.

Sophie looked up at her sister. "Um, you did."

"Did I?" Hayley turned to Kim and giggled. "Well, then I take it back. Because guess what? When Sam found out I liked him, he decided that he liked me back!"

She waved a piece of paper. It was folded up tight. "It's all in this note!" she said. "So really, you made my life better. Thanks, Sophie!"

Wow.

That was not something Sophie thought she would hear. Ever. The truth was her sister didn't thank her much. And she *never* thanked her in front of Kim.

Sophie got a feeling inside her. It was like when the sky was cloudy and the sun suddenly came out.

Sophie the Honest had made the world better! Her shoulders felt a little lighter. Her eyes didn't burn so much.

Then Kate climbed onto the bus. She walked by without a word and sat as far away from Sophie as she could.

The bus lurched forward and Sophie's heart began to pound. She got another feeling, like the clouds had just come back. And now it was raining. Hard.

So what if the world was a better place for Hayley? For Sophie, it was worse. Honestly, it was no fun being Sophie the Honest all alone.

Then again, she wasn't alone. Ella was beside her.

Ella grabbed Sophie's arm and tugged it. "Can

you come play again today?" she asked. Sophie sighed. Yes. She could. And as Sophie the Honest, she should say so. But the truth was she just plain didn't want to.

Then, all of a sudden, a big thought hit Sophie. *Bam!* She had been honest to everyone else . . . but she had been lying to herself.

The truth was she didn't really *want* to be Sophie the Honest anymore!

She didn't want to answer every question. Every time.

She didn't want to stop pretending. For the rest of her life.

She didn't want to have to tell secrets. Not when she promised not to, at least.

And she didn't want to hurt people's feelings. There was nothing worse than that!

What Sophie really wanted, more than anything else, was to be Kate's best friend.

"So?" Ella tugged some more. "Can you play? Can you?"

Sophie looked down. She shook her head.

"No. I'm sorry, Ella. I can't play today," Sophie said. "I have something important to do."

And that was not a lie at all. That was the truth.

☆ ☆ ☆

When the bus reached Sophie's stop, she got off. But she didn't head home.

She said good-bye to Ella. And she waved to Hayley and Kim. Then she stood by the curb and waited for Kate.

As soon as Kate saw her, she frowned and walked by without a word. But Sophie was expecting that. She ran to catch her.

"Kate! Wait for me! I have to talk to you," she called.

Kate stopped and turned around. She crossed her arms. "Go ahead."

Sophie took a deep breath. She had so much to say she wasn't sure where to begin.

"I want to say that I'm sorry, Kate. Really, really sorry. And I'm not just saying that because I want to ride a horse. Even though it is my lifelong dream. But I'm sorry I was such a big mouth. I didn't mean to make everyone mad or hurt anyone's feelings. And I won't let you down again. You can trust me. I promise. You're my best friend in the whole world! Honest!"

Kate's mouth had been a straight line. Slowly it curved into a grin.

Yes! Sophie could feel it. They were going to be friends again!

"Cross your heart, Sophie the Honest?" Kate asked.

Sophie smiled and crossed her heart again and again.

Then she reached out her arms. So did Kate. They hugged.

Ouch!

Sophie jumped back. This time her broach really did stick her!

Sophie took it off, dropped it into her backpack, and let out a big sigh. A happy one this time. Then she bit her lip. "Honestly, Kate, I don't know if Sophie the Honest is *me*," she said.

Kate put her finger to her chin. "Well, there's always Sophie the Chatterbox," she teased.

Sophie rolled her eyes. "Thanks, but no thanks!" she said.

"Then what?" Kate asked.

Sophie shrugged. She wanted a great name, but she didn't know what yet. Oh, well. She would think of something. What mattered more right then was that she had her best friend back.

(*And* that she didn't have to tell a grown-up every single thing she did at school ever again!)

But what about Kate? Sophie wondered. Were the other girls still mad at her?

Then Kate told Sophie something that made her feel even better. She had talked to Mrs. Belle. She was going to ask her daughter if Kate could bring more friends to the horse farm.

Hopefully, everyone could go. Including Sophie!

(And hopefully everyone would forget the not-so-great things she had said.)

Sophie was feeling so much better. She kicked

a rock and watched it bounce away. And that was when she saw...

There in the grass. Was it a dollar?

Sophie looked a little closer.

Yes! It was!

Or... no. It had a number five on it.

It was a five-dollar bill! Sophie had never found one of those before!

She bent down and picked it up. And then she saw the zero. A five *and* a zero!

"Look, Kate!" She held it up. "A fifty! I'm rich!"

Then Sophie looked at Kate. And Kate looked at her.

"Are you thinking what I'm thinking?" Sophie asked.

"I think so!" Kate said.

Sophie the Rich! Now that was a good name!

No, wait—Sophie the *Zillionaire*!

Yes! That was even better!

So maybe SOPHIE hasn't found the perfect
name...but she isn't giving up yet!

Take a peek at Sophie's next adventure....

Sophie stared at the thing in her hand. She turned it over carefully. It was paper and green, and it had the number fifty all over it.

That was because it was fifty whole dollars!

Sophie could not believe it.

"I can't believe it!" she said to Kate Barry, who was standing beside her. Kate was Sophie's very best friend. "It's fifty whole dollars!"

Sophie looked down at the grass next to the sidewalk. That was where she had picked up the fifty-dollar bill. She hoped that there was even more money there! But there was not.

Still. She had fifty whole dollars. She was probably the richest girl in the whole world!

(Well ... maybe she wasn't richer than a

princess. But she was richer than any ordinary girl in Ordinary, Virginia, she bet!)

Sophie wanted so badly to be special. Now she really was! And to think, all she had to do was look down as she walked home from the bus stop.

"Where do you think it came from?" Kate asked her, as they started to walk.

Sophie shrugged. "I don't know."

Then she got a feeling. It was not so good. For Sophie to find money, someone else must have lost it first. But there was no one else around.

Sophie started to feel better. There wasn't anybody to ask. Plus didn't her big sister, Hayley, always say, "Finders keepers, losers sweepers"?

Sophie wasn't sure why losers had to sweep. But that was their problem. The fifty dollars was hers!

"So what are you going to do with it?" Kate asked. She grinned and licked her lips. "I think you should buy lots of gum!"

Sophie knew that Kate liked gum. A lot. This was mostly because her mom did not buy it—not since Kate chewed some, then put it behind her ear to keep it. It worked for a girl in a movie they saw. But it did not work for Kate. It got stuck in her hair, and her mom had to cut a bunch of it off. Kate looked funny for a while. But she still liked gum just as much, after all that.

Sophie thought about gum for a minute, then shook her head. "I'm going to keep the money. And tomorrow at school I'm going to tell everyone about it," she said.

Sophie could picture the kids in her class. They would be amazed that she was so rich. They would never call her just plain Sophie... or Sophie M.... or even Sophie Miller again!